At first all Babs could manage to do was gasp for breath and wave the stack of printouts. But finally she caught her breath enough to squeeze out, "Emergency! Some kind of big crime is coming down on the Internet!"

Brother took a quick look at the Huff and Puff printouts. "I don't know what this is about. But it looks serious. Come on! We've got to show this to Teacher Bob."

But the bell hadn't rung yet and the door safety wouldn't let them in. "But it's an emergency!" cried Babs.

"What sort of emergency?" said the door safety.

"It's going to be an emergency for your nose if you don't let us in," said Too-Tall. The door safety let them in.

"What's going on?" demanded Teacher Bob as the gang stormed into the room.

BIG CHAPTER BOOKS

The Berenstain Bears
LOST IN CYBERSPACE

by the Berenstains

A BIG CHAPTER BOOK™

Random House New York

www.randomhouse.com/kids
www.berenstainbears.com

Library of Congress Cataloging-in-Publication Data
Berenstain, Stan, 1923–
The Berenstain Bears lost in cyberspace / Stan & Jan Berenstain.
  p. cm.— (Big chapter books)
Summary: When Brother Bear and his classmates get laptop computers as a school experiment, they become lost in cyberspace, cruising chat rooms, exchanging e-mail, clicking onto web sites, and neglecting their friends and family.
ISBN: 0-679-88946-9 (trade) — ISBN: 0-679-98946-3 (lib.bdg.)
[1. Internet (Computer network)—Fiction. 2. Computers—Fiction. 3. Schools—Fiction. 4. Bears—Fiction.] I. Berenstain, Jan, 1923–
II. Title. III. Series: Berenstain, Stan, 1923– Big chapter book.
PZ7.B4483Bersg   1999 [Fic]—dc21 98-46400

Printed in the United States of America   10 9 8 7 6 5 4 3 2 1

BIG CHAPTER BOOKS is a trademark of Berenstain Enterprises, Inc.

Contents

Chapter 1
An Experiment

The cubs of Teacher Bob's class were all abuzz as they settled into their seats one fall morning. They had come to school expecting that their classroom would look no different from the way it had looked the day before (or the day before that). But different it did look. *Very* different.

Usually the cubs' desktops were clear, except maybe for a stray pen or pencil someone had forgotten to put away the day before. But today not a single desktop was clear. On each sat an object that few of the cubs recognized.

In the back row, Barry Bruin lifted the part that looked like a lid and saw a keyboard. "What *is* this thing? A typewriter?" he asked Harry McGill, whose wheelchair was parked next to him.

"Nah," said Harry. "We had typing last year, remember? It's a laptop computer." Harry was a real computer whiz. He was as handy with his home computer as he was with the electric wheelchairs he'd used since he was a small cub.

"Well, if it's a *lap*top computer," said Barry, who was the class jokester, "then why is it on my *desk*?"

"Just so you could make that dumb joke," said Harry without cracking a smile.

Too-Tall Grizzly laughed and said, "Good one, Wheels." His gang snickered.

Teacher Bob was raising the venetian blinds in the back of the room and overheard Barry. "Barry wants to know why these computers are called laptops," he said. "That's because they're battery-powered and small enough to fit on your lap if necessary."

"The only thing allowed to sit on my lap is my girlfriend, Queenie," said Too-Tall. Too-Tall's gang, who had to laugh at Too-Tall's wisecracks if they knew what was good for them, laughed noisily. Queenie turned and made a nasty face at Too-Tall. She and Too-Tall had an on-again, off-again thing that was off at the moment.

"Pipe down, you two," said Teacher Bob. "We've got a lot of ground to cover, and…"

"Good morning, ladies and germs," interrupted jokester Barry Bruin, jumping to his feet. "Say, if we've got a lot of ground to cover, why are we sitting here in a stuffy classroom when we could go outside and cover it?"

"Sit down, Barry," said Teacher Bob.

"But, Teacher Bob," said Barry, "how am I ever going to be a stand-up comic if you keep telling me to sit down?"

Everyone in the class turned to Barry and said, "SIT DOWN!"

Barry sat down.

"As I said," continued Teacher Bob, "they're called laptops. Why are they on your desks? I'll tell you why. You cubs have been chosen for an experiment."

Queenie McBear's hand shot up.

"Yes, Queenie?" said Teacher Bob.

"Who chose us to be guinea pigs in an experiment?" she asked. "My mom says cubs can't be used in experiments without their parents' permission."

Teacher Bob smiled. "But, Queenie, this isn't a *medical* experiment or a *psychology* experiment," he said. "It's just an ordinary school experiment. We do them all the time. Why, every time I try to teach you cubs something, it's an experiment."

Ferdy, the class genius, pointed his thumb in the direction of the Too-Tall Gang and whispered a little too loudly to Trudy, his genius girlfriend, "In certain cases, it's a *failed experiment.*"

"Oh, yeah, you nerd-faced twerp?" threatened Too-Tall, waving a big fist. "I'm gonna hit you on the head so hard you'll be looking out through your belt buckle."

Teacher Bob didn't say anything. He just turned toward Too-Tall and made his "that's enough" face. Teacher Bob was a very good, patient teacher who got along with his cubs. But when he made his "that's enough" face, they knew fun time was over.

"As I was saying before I was interrupted, we experiment all the time. Every time we try something out to see if it will work, that's a kind of experiment."

"So we're gonna try these computers out to see if they work?" said Barry. "What are we, computer testers?"

"No," said Teacher Bob. "Actually, the computers will be testing *us*, in a way. This all started when Squire Grizzly, Bonnie

Brown's uncle, bought Bonnie a laptop computer." He nodded at Bonnie, who blushed. "Bonnie has always been a good student, but after just a couple of months with her new computer, Bonnie's grades went from good to great."

"Almost as great as mine," said Ferdy Factual. Trudy Brunowitz elbowed him in the ribs and shushed him.

"Thank you for sharing that, Ferdy," said Teacher Bob. The class tittered. "Anyway, the squire decided that Bonnie wasn't just doing better in school but was learning more outside school, too. You know, there's even more information on the Internet now than there is in the entire school library—much more. And that information is much easier to get at than the information stored in the library."

As Teacher Bob went on about how great

computers were, Brother Bear's mind wandered over to where Bonnie Brown was sitting, blushing. *So that's what's been going on,* thought Brother. *She's run off with a computer.* He'd hardly seen Bonnie at all over the past few weeks. They were pretty good friends, not boyfriend and girlfriend, but good friends nonetheless. Brother and Bonnie took long walks together. They met at the movies sometimes and sat together away from the gang. Sometimes they even held hands. But they hadn't done any of that for a while. So that was why! Bonnie wasn't angry with him or anything. She'd been "lost in cyberspace." *What a relief,* thought Brother. He was confident he could compete with a dopey laptop computer.

But Brother shouldn't have been so confident. He and his whole group would soon find out that computers have a strange power. The power to pull cubs into another

world. The world of cyberspace. And they would find out that it was a fascinating world; a world of endless information. A world of exciting computer games. A world that reached to the farthest ends of Bear Country—and if you weren't careful, sometimes it could be a world of deadly danger.

. "Oh, Brother," said Teacher Bob. "Would you care to rejoin us?" Teacher Bob had an uncanny ability to see minds wandering off.

"Huh?" said Brother. "Oh, sure."

"Good to have you back," said Teacher Bob. "Now, just to sum up: Squire Grizzly thought it would be an interesting experiment to provide all the students of one class with computers that can be used both in school and at home. He's sure they will raise your grades and help you learn faster."

"What do *you* think, Teacher Bob?" asked Brother Bear.

"I think so too," said Teacher Bob, "but I'm not as sure as the squire is."

"Why not?" said Cousin Fred. "It worked for Bonnie, didn't it?"

"That's true," admitted Teacher Bob. "But that only proves it worked for *Bonnie*. Your principal, Mr. Honeycomb, and I agree that before Squire Grizzly donates computers to all the students in Bear Country School, an experiment should be tried on a group of cubs—a group large enough to give us a good idea of how well the whole student body will do with computers. Doesn't that make sense?"

"I guess so," said Queenie. "But I still feel like a guinea pig."

"You *look* like a guinea pig!" cracked Too-Tall with a big grin.

"Oh, yeah?" said Queenie. "Well, you look like a different kind of pig—a big old

ugly farm pig that eats garbage and says, 'Oink! Oink!' "

"But you didn't let me finish," protested Too-Tall. "I think guinea pigs are cute and adorable—can't we kiss and make up?"

"Well, we can make up," said Queenie, who couldn't help smiling. "But forget about kissing!"

"That's quite enough of *that*," warned Teacher Bob. "Now, quiet down. We'll spend all day today getting to know our new computers. Although they belong to the school, you may think of them as your own for the next month. You may store all your homework and exams on them. The squire is having printers delivered to each of your homes this afternoon so that you can start printing out your homework assignments right away. Squire Grizzly has also provided each computer with educational software. You also have e-mail—that's electronic mail."

"Are these laptops Internet-connected?" asked Ferdy.

"Absolutely," said Teacher Bob. That got a rise out of the class. Most of the class had heard about the Internet and were eager to try it.

"Hey, cool!" said Queenie. "My older cousin, Bermuda, loves the Internet. She says you can meet guys that way."

"Hey!" said Too-Tall. "You've already got a guy!"

Teacher Bob had one "that's enough"

look left. He turned it on Queenie and Too-Tall, and they simmered down.

"What folks call the Information Super-highway is a wonderful and exciting thing," said Teacher Bob. "And while it's not brand-new, it's new enough so that no one knows what it will mean to all of us. But I've been on-line for more than a year and I can tell you this. It has great potential for learning. On the other hand…"

"Excuse me, Teacher Bob," interrupted Ferdy.

"Yes, Ferdy?"

"I feel that I must point out to you," said Ferdy as Trudy rolled her eyes, "that hardly anyone calls it the Information Superhigh-way anymore. The new term is cyberspace."

"All right, Ferdy," said Teacher Bob. "Then cyberspace it is. Now, if you'll all open your laptops, we'll blast off."

Chapter 2
Hail the Internet

Teacher Bob's pupils were really excited about the idea of exploring cyberspace with their new "spaceships." Except, perhaps, for Brother, who already was jealous of Bonnie's laptop. But even he was excited about the idea of getting on the Internet. He'd heard that you could type in a word and get all kinds of information about that word. The word Brother was going to type in was "sports." Brother loved sports. He loved playing sports. Especially baseball. He was also a big baseball trivia fan. Maybe the

Internet would help him beat Cousin Fred at baseball trivia. He'd do the homework assignment, of course. It was simple enough. They were to write a statement on the future of computers and print it out. How long could that take?

In fact, Brother had a date to play baseball with Cousin Fred and Barry Bruin that afternoon. But when he set up his laptop in his room, it looked so inviting that he wanted to try it. He looked at the instruction book. It was so complicated that he called up Harry McGill, the class computer expert, to find out how to get on the Internet. Of course, Harry's phone was busy. Brother realized right away that everybody was calling Harry for help. Finally, he got through to Harry, who told him exactly how to get on the Internet. And it worked!

"Brother!" called Sister from the bottom

of the stairs. "Aren't we supposed to play baseball over at Cousin Fred's today?" Since there was no answer, she climbed the stairs and went into Brother's room. He was huddled over the computer. "I heard your whole class got laptops. How about that? But you promised to teach me how to throw a curve today." No answer from Brother. He remained huddled over the computer. As he worked the keyboard and the mouse, long lists of baseball statistics appeared on the screen. More baseball statistics than Brother had ever dreamed of.

It looked to Sister as if Brother was hypnotized by the computer. His eyes had that glazed-over look. Sister put her hand between Brother and the computer screen and moved it up and down. Still no reaction from Brother. "Oh, well," said Sister as she headed downstairs. "Guess I'm going to find out what it's like being an only cub."

The members of Teacher Bob's class had a great time that evening getting the feel of their laptops, exchanging e-mail, and checking out web sites. But it was the chat rooms that really captured their imaginations. Chat rooms were amazing things. They were imaginary rooms where you could enter and "chat" with anyone else in the room. You chatted by typing words and sentences which instantly appeared on the screen, and then others did the same thing and their words and sentences also appeared on the screen.

There were *all kinds* of chat rooms. Sports chat rooms, science chat rooms, movie chat rooms, fashion chat rooms, chat rooms for just about anything you could think of.

It didn't take Brother too long to find a sports chat room. While Queenie was searching for the "Guys and Girls" chat room that her older cousin Bermuda had told her about, she found one she liked even better: the Giddy Gossip chat room. And jokester Barry Bruin was in "bad joke heaven" when he found the Comedy Club chat room. Young poet Babs Bruno, who was kind of snobby about computers because she didn't think they were "artistic," found the perfect chat room: the Young Poets chat room. Teacher Bob's laptoppers got so deep into chat rooms that they were almost lost in cyberspace when they all got an e-mail from Teacher Bob. This is what it said:

```
Calling all laptoppers.
Don't forget your homework!
```

They knew the e-mail was from Teacher Bob because it was signed with his web site address, www.teachbob.edu.

Most of them got to work on their homework.

Chapter 3
Rules of the Cyberspace Road

"Good morning, class," said Teacher Bob. "Bonnie, will you please collect the homework?"

"Hey, Teach," said Too-Tall, "I couldn't bring my homework in."

"Why is that, Too-Tall?" said Teacher Bob. "Did your dog eat it?"

"I don't even *have* a dog, Teach," said Too-Tall. "No, my printer got jammed. In fact, that happened to my whole gang. Their printers got jammed."

"Oh?" said Teacher Bob, trying to keep his temper.

"Yeah," said Too-Tall. "I guess it's one of them co-inky-dinks."

Teacher Bob took a deep breath and began looking through the homework. "Well," he said, smiling, "I see you've all become great spellers overnight. I don't suppose the fact that all your laptops have spellcheckers has anything to do with that. Hmm, some of these look pretty good."

As Teacher Bob looked over the homework, two things struck him. One was that each cub saw the value of computers from his or her own point of view. He could have easily guessed who'd written them even if they hadn't been signed. Sports fan Brother's statement was about sports. Poetry fan Babs's was about poetry. Would-be comic Barry's was in the form of a joke.

That didn't surprise Teacher Bob. In fact, it confirmed one of his fears: Instead of widening the cubs' interests, computers just strengthened the interests they already had.

But there was good news, too. Teacher Bob was pleased that many members of the class had figured out how to use the design and graphics software that came with the laptops. This is what some of the homework looked like:

I think computers have a great future because they know everything there is to know about sports. Sports trivia, anyone?

Brother Bear

Computers have a great future because all the great poetry is on-line.

Babs Bruno

I think computers have a great future because a computer is an encyclopedia and a dictionary all rolled into one (of course, if you can't type, you're in big trouble).

Cousin Fred

We think computers have a great future because they are almost as smart as we are.

Ferdy Factual and
Trudy Brunowitz

I think computers have a great future because you can make jokes about them.
Sample: Where does your laptop go when you stand up?
Answer: On the floor, stupid.

Barry Bruin
(available for parties and bear mitzvahs)

"There's another thing I want to talk to you about," said Teacher Bob, "and it's something very serious. Chat rooms are great fun and an exciting way to exchange ideas with cubs from all over Bear Country, but sometimes chat rooms can be dangerous."

"Dangerous?" said Brother. "How so?"

"Yeah," said Babs, "I found a great chat room. It's called Young Poets. I don't see how *that* can be dangerous."

"That's what's dangerous about it—all that crummy poetry!" said Too-Tall.

"Too-Tall," said Babs grandly, "you have no soul."

"Have, too," Too-Tall shot back. "Two of 'em, on the bottoms of my big feet." He put his feet up on his desk for emphasis. "Ha! Ha! Ha!"

"That's a good one, Chief," said Skuzz.

"Feet on the floor, please," said Teacher Bob. "All right, now listen carefully and I'll explain how cyberspace can be dangerous." The class calmed down and listened.

"As you know," continued Teacher Bob, "you don't use real names in chat rooms." Some members of the class had already joined chat rooms and chosen nicknames. They started calling them out.

"I'm Allsports," said Brother.

"I'm Mad Joker," said Barry.

"I'm The Hammer," said Too-Tall, hitting his desk with a hard fist.

"Okay," continued Teacher Bob, "and

what are some of the nicknames you noticed on the different chat rooms?"

"I've noticed 'Dawn' and 'Miss Muse' on the Young Poets chat room," said Babs.

"There's 'Giggle Guy' and 'Charlie Chuckles' on the Comedy Club chat room," said Barry.

"My buddies on the Macho chat room are 'Smash Mouth' and 'Knuckles,'" said Too-Tall.

"What, pray tell," said Ferdy, "does one chat about on the Macho chat room?"

"We chat about wiping up the schoolyard with nerd-faced twerps like you."

"Should I pop him, Chief?" said Skuzz, Too-Tall's second in command.

"Calm down," said Teacher Bob. "I said this was serious. Babs, tell me something about this Miss Muse. What do you think she's like?"

"I suppose she's a girl like me who's interested in poetry," said Babs.

"But how do you *know* that's who she is?" asked Teacher Bob. Babs and the rest of the class were beginning to get the message.

"I guess I don't, really," said Babs.

"That's my point," said Teacher Bob. "For all you know, Miss Muse might be a dangerous grown-up criminal who plans to make

friends with you and lure you out to some dark place and cubnap you."

"I'd like to see him try!" said Babs. "My dad happens to be chief of police, and he'd…" But she did look a little frightened.

"Now, I'm not saying that's going to happen," said Teacher Bob. "In fact, most of the cubs you'll meet in cyberspace are exactly who they say they are: cubs like you who are interested in chatting about sports, poetry, and the like. But that sort of thing *can* happen. It's just that I want you to keep security in mind when you choose chat room nicknames. But there's a lot more to computer security than that. I've put it all together in this. It's called 'Rules of the Cyberspace Road.' Would you please hand these out, Bonnie?"

The class members read the handout carefully. This is what it said:

RULES OF THE CYBERSPACE ROAD

1. Never tell a chat room "pal" your real name, phone number, address, or which school you go to.

2. Use your chat room name when exchanging e-mail with chat room buddies.

3. You may use your real name when exchanging e-mail, but only with those you know personally (schoolmates, friends, neighbors, relatives).

4. Never agree to meet with a chat room pal without your parents' permission.

5. If you do plan to meet with a chat room or e-mail pal, a parent or trusted grownup must go with you.

"Rules of the Cyberspace Road" put a bit of a damper on the cubs' excitement about cyberspace. But not for long. As the school day came to a close, the class was raring to get back to those wild, swinging chat rooms. Brother was closing up his laptop and getting ready to head for home when Bonnie Brown came over to him. "Hi, Brother," she said.

"Hi, Bonnie," said Brother.

"Brother, I hope you understand why I haven't been around much lately," said Bonnie. "It was this laptop experiment. It was my uncle's idea to keep it a secret until he

made his decision about buying our whole class laptops."

"Oh, I understand," said Brother. "I really do."

"So how about walking home together and maybe coming over so we can do our homework together tonight?" asked Bonnie.

"Walking home together is fine," said Brother, snapping his laptop shut. "But there's a big trivia contest on the sports chat room and they're counting on me. Tell you what, though, here's a pack of quiz cards. Test me on them while we walk home."

Bonnie wasn't exactly thrilled with the idea, but she went along. Bonnie read off questions and Brother answered them.

"What ballplayer hit the most home runs in a single season, and how many did he hit?" asked Bonnie.

"Mark McGrizzly. He hit 70," said Brother.

"What pitcher had the lowest earned run average over his whole career?" said Bonnie.

"Sandy Bearfax," said Brother.

And so it went until they came to where their paths parted. "Gee, thanks for drilling me," said Brother as he took off down the road.

"Hmm," said Bonnie. "I'm not so sure this whole laptop thing was such a good idea."

Chapter 4
Wall-to-Wall Chat Rooms

When Brother got home, he hurried upstairs to set up his laptop for the sports trivia wars. But Sister, who had already gotten home, was in his room waiting for him. "Hi, Brother," she said. "We just started long division and I'm behind already."

"Maybe later, Sis," said Brother. He was already at his laptop, clicking and double-clicking like crazy. "I've signed up for a big baseball trivia contest on the sports chat room tonight, and I've got a lot of boning up to do."

"Well, that's just great!" said Sister as she left the room. "Having an older brother is annoying enough, but having one who won't help you with long division is *really* uncool!"

The same sort of thing was happening all over the neighborhood. The members of Teacher Bob's laptop class were cruising chat rooms, exchanging e-mail, clicking onto web sites. The class had history and geography homework that evening. Some of the new laptoppers even used the on-line encyclopedia for homework reference.

When Babs got home, she showed her dad, Chief of Police Bruno, Teacher Bob's "Rules of the Cyberspace Road." Babs knew that her dad had been using computers in his police work for years. He was even hooked into the Big Bear City computer network, which covered the whole country.

"Good for Teacher Bob," said Chief Bruno. "Just follow these rules and you'll be fine. The fact is that computer crime is getting to be a big thing. All kinds of stuff is going on. They're even putting a special computer crime team together up in Big Bear City..." There was nothing the chief liked to talk about more than crime. But being a good dad, he noticed when Babs started shifting from one foot to the other. "Hey, I know you're eager to get into that Poets chat room, so get going."

"Thanks, Dad," said Babs. She zipped up to her room and set up her laptop. Babs was an excellent student who always did her homework first thing. That evening, however, she made very short work of her homework. She could hardly wait to get in on the action on the Young Poets chat room.

But first she had to think up a good chat room nickname. She wanted to think up a "safe" nickname, of course. Since it was a poetry chat room and since poetry was about words and sounds, she didn't want to use something dopey or clunky. As she looked around her room for ideas, she saw Puff, her old teddy, whom she still slept

with—though nobody, but nobody, except her mom and dad knew it. "What do you think, Puff?" she said, half to Puff and half to herself. "How about 'Puff' for a chat room name?"

Babs had named the teddy Puff because "The Three Little Pigs and the Big Bad Wolf" had been her favorite bedtime story when she was a little cub. She logged on to the Young Poets chat room and called up the instructions on how to join and register a name. Babs had a number of poems she wanted to present.

Teacher Bob and her friends Bonnie and Queenie liked Babs's poems a lot. But Babs wanted to try them out in the wider world. She wanted to know what other young poets thought of her work. The Young Poets chat room crowd could be a tough audience. Babs had noticed that the night before when she first logged on. She was becoming more and more nervous as she waited for her name to be accepted. But surprise, surprise! It wasn't accepted. "Choose other name. 'Puff' already taken!" said the screen.

How strange, thought Babs. But she figured, "Oh well," and set to work thinking up another name. She decided to go back to the Three Little Pigs and try "Huff." But "Huff" didn't work either! "Choose other name. 'Huff' already taken!" said the screen.

How discouraging! But she'd heard that poets have to get used to rejection, so she thought up another name. This time she went back to her second-favorite bedtime story, "Goldiebear and the Three People," and chose "Goldiebear." This time there was no comment from the screen, so after some more clicks, Babs was a member in

good standing of the Young Poets chat room under the name "Goldiebear."

Finally, she was ready to present her first poem to the Young Poets chat room. It was almost like getting published, and she was nervous about it. But which poem should it be? Babs wrote all kinds of poems. Haiku was one of her specialties. It had strict rules. To be accepted as haiku, a poem had to have exactly three lines and seventeen syllables. Babs had one called "Fog."

FOG

Silent gray mist
Coming going leaving wet grass
and puddles on rocks

And she had another one called "Lady-bug." Perhaps that would be a better choice.

LADYBUG

A six-legged four-winged
black-spotted busy buzzy
bright orange button

While Babs was trying to decide which

poem to post on the Young Poets chat room, her laptop classmates were clicking away on their own machines. Ferdy was over at Trudy's place, where the two of them were cruising science chat rooms. Ferdy and Trudy were caught up in the hot scientific argument about whether birds had descended from dinosaurs. Trudy was in favor of the bird theory and Ferdy was against it. The argument got pretty hot and heavy—not only in the chat rooms, but also face to face.

Just up the road at the McBear home, Queenie had a visitor. It was her cousin, Bermuda, who was quite a bit older than Queenie. She was very much into guys and was even allowed to date. Bermuda had been on-line for years and was looking over Queenie's shoulder as she checked out her favorite teen chat rooms and web sites. "Let me sit in for a minute," said Bermuda. "I'll show you some real action." She took over Queenie's seat and after a few keystrokes, they were logged on to "Big Date!"—the hottest dating service in cyberspace.

"Oh, I don't think so," said Queenie. "It goes against Teacher Bob's rules…"

"Will you relax?" said Bermuda. "We're not gonna date anybody, we're just gonna have a little fun."

Chapter 5
Another Co-Inky-Dink

The next morning, Teacher Bob was in his classroom setting up for the day's work. The first thing on the schedule was laptop discussion. Following would be a schedule of regular schoolwork. The big event of the day was going to be a surprise quiz. It was a combined history and geography quiz. It was tied in pretty closely to the previous night's homework. Teacher Bob didn't give many surprise quizzes. He didn't think they were quite fair. But, on the other hand, he figured that the cubs who didn't do their homework deserved what they got.

As for the laptop experiment, Teacher Bob was all for it if it helped cubs with their education. Teacher Bob liked cubs and he liked teaching them. He had a habit of standing at the window and looking out as the whole schoolyard of cubs formed up for class when the bell rang. It was easy picking out his cubs. Brother Bear was usually playing ball with Cousin Fred. Queenie was usually telling the latest gossip to her buddies Bonnie Brown and Babs Bruno. Barry Bruin was usually trying his latest bad joke on some poor unfortunate. Too-Tall and his gang were usually swaggering through the schoolyard frightening kindergartners.

But not today. Today, the members of Teacher Bob's class looked like a bunch of little lawyers carrying briefcases. Only they weren't briefcases, they were laptops. And

when the bell rang and all the different classes lined up, Teacher Bob's class looked like the law firm of Laptop, Laptop, Laptop, Laptop, Laptop, and Laptop.

"All right, settle down, class!" said Teacher Bob as his cubs rumbled into the room. "All right," he continued, "let's get 'laptop discussion' out of the way first. Any new business?"

Barry jumped up and said, "Got tons of jokes!"

"Your jokes don't come under the heading of new business," said Brother, "they come under the heading of old business. Old, old, old business!"

"But how am I ever going to be a stand-up comic if everybody keeps telling me to…"

"SIT DOWN!" roared the class.

"I've got an announcement to make," said Too-Tall. "I'm changing my chat room personality. I'm no longer The Hammer. I am now Mr. Smooth." All eyes turned to Too-Tall's girlfriend, Queenie, for a reaction, but Queenie didn't seem to have heard. It was as if she were somewhere else.

"Too-Tall," said Ferdy, "you're about as smooth as rocky road ice cream without the ice cream."

I AM NOW MR. SMOOTH.

"That's all right, little fellow," said Too-Tall. "My former self, The Hammer, would have popped you for that remark, but that sort of thing just rolls right off Mr. Smooth." The class got a laugh out of that. Except for Babs, who seemed to have something on her mind. She raised her hand.

"Yes, Babs," said Teacher Bob.

"Well," said Babs. "The weirdest thing happened last night when I tried to enter the name I chose on the Young Poets chat room. I chose 'Puff'—never mind why—and the screen said, 'Choose other name. "Puff" already taken!' "

"Strange," said Teacher Bob, "but not exactly weird."

"But when I switched to 'Huff,' the exact same thing happened. The screen said, 'Choose other name. "Huff" already taken!' " said Babs. "Don't you think that's weird?"

"I suppose so," said Teacher Bob. "But you have to understand how vast cyberspace is. When you go on-line, there are thousands and thousands of other young poets out there, any of whom might have chosen those names. So I don't think it's a problem."

"Yeah," said Too-Tall. "Don't worry about it. It's just another one of those co-inky-dinks."

"The word, my brain-dead friend," said Ferdy with a yawn, "is *coincidence.*"

"Should I pop him, Chief?" asked Vinnie.

"Let it pass," said Too-Tall.

"The word, as Ferdy points out," said Teacher Bob, "is *coincidence.* Definition please, Cousin Fred."

"*Coincidence,*" said Fred, who read the dictionary and the encyclopedia just for fun. "When two or more things happen at the

THE WORD, MY BRAIN-DEAD FRIEND, IS COINCIDENCE.

same time by mere chance, it's called a coincidence."

"Of course, coincidences happen all the time," said Teacher Bob. "And most of them are ordinary everyday coincidences. We've all had the experience of running into somebody you didn't expect to see at the supermarket or the Burger Bear. Or when you're about to call somebody on the phone, the phone rings and it's the person you were about to call."

But that wasn't the whole story about coincidences. Some weren't ordinary at all. And while they didn't happen very often, some coincidences, like Bab's Huff and Puff experience in cyberspace, could turn out to be downright dangerous.

Chapter 6
Drop-Dead Downtown
Sensational

"How do you like living dangerously?" Bermuda asked Queenie.

"I guess it's exciting," said Queenie. "But I'm not sure I like it." Queenie was pretty bold compared to her friends Bonnie Brown and Babs Bruno, but not compared to her older cousin.

"Relax," said Bermuda. The two of them were up in Bermuda's room, where Queenie was getting a makeover for her big computer date.

"I don't know why I can't wear my regular clothes," protested Queenie.

"Don't be ridiculous," said Bermuda. "Here, take off those little-girl earrings and put on these hoops. And that clear nail polish just won't do. Let me do your nails with my purple polish."

"Gee, I don't know," said Queenie.

"Look," said Bermuda, "make up your mind. If you're gonna date older guys, you're gonna have to dress older, make up older, and think older."

Queenie sighed and sat quietly as Bermuda finished her nails. The older guy she was going to meet later at the Pizza Shack was probably a sharp dresser and all that went with it. "Why can't we meet at the Burger Bear?" she asked. "That's where I usually hang out."

"Because that's where the younger crowd hangs out," said Bermuda, finishing up the last purple nail. "Okay, done." She pulled Queenie over to a full-length mirror. "Have a look at yourself."

Queenie looked in the mirror. The person looking back at her was wearing one of Bermuda's shifts, a pair of her stretch pants, a bunch of jewelry, and purple fingernail polish. If she'd met that person, she probably wouldn't have recognized her. "What do you think?" she asked nervously.

"I think you look drop-dead downtown sensational," said Bermuda. "Now, come on. We've got to head over to the Pizza Shack for your date."

Queenie held back a little.

"There's nothing to worry about," said Bermuda. "You'll be with me. Everybody knows me over at the Pizza Shack. I'll probably even know the guy."

Queenie took a deep breath and followed Bermuda out into the scary night air.

Chapter 7
Computers—
Good News or Bad News?

Brother Bear and Bonnie Brown didn't need a computer dating service to get together again. They just took up where they had left off. Except that now they had one more thing in common: their laptops. They were partnering on a special assignment Teacher Bob had given them. They were to do a report on the subject "Computers—Good News or Bad News?"

On the way home from school, Brother had given Sister a message that he was going home with Bonnie so they could work on a homework assignment together. Now they were set up in Squire Grizzly's study. It was a tricky subject and they were trying to get started by talking back and forth on the subject. "There's no question that computers are great for looking up stuff—baseball statistics, for example," said Brother.

"And just about anything else, for that matter," said Bonnie.

"You know something?" said Brother. "This may be bad news about computers—I haven't played a minute of real baseball since your uncle gave out the laptops."

"You could play computer baseball," said Bonnie.

"It isn't the same. Computer baseball is

all typing and mouse clicks. Real baseball is grass-stained baseballs, facing a tough pitcher, and getting dirty in a headfirst slide."

"That's good stuff," said Bonnie. "Maybe we can work it into our report."

They had started getting into the subject earlier on the way to Grizzly Mansion. But when the mansion had come into view,

Brother just stared. Great Grizzly Mansion always affected Brother that way. It was an amazing place—the grandest home in all Bear Country. It was more like a castle than a home. It had statues and fountains, towers and turrets. Brother had been there many, many times when he was little and Sister was even littler. Their dad, who was just about the best woodworker in Bear Coun-

try, used to take him and Sister with him when he went there to work on Squire and Lady Grizzly's priceless antique furniture. "Heck, all it needs is a moat," Brother had said as they came to the gate.

"Uncle's building one," said Bonnie.

"Building one what?" asked Brother.

"A moat," said Bonnie.

"You've got to be kidding!" said Brother.

"Not at all," said Bonnie. "As a matter of fact, it's almost done."

Brother looked. The squire had built one all around the mansion. It didn't have a drawbridge or anything. It wasn't all that noticeable since it was hidden by shrubs. But it was a moat all right.

"My uncle is very security-minded," Bonnie explained. "He has a good reason to be. While he's a darling at home, he's a very tough businessbear. You don't get to be the

richest bear in Bear Country without making some enemies."

"I guess not," said Brother.

"And that doesn't even count all the robbers out there looking to steal his valuable antiques and priceless paintings."

"I guess not," said Brother as he and Bonnie walked up the path to the front door, where the butler was waiting to let them in.

Brother and Bonnie had finally gotten started on their report, but all they had done was the first paragraph. Bonnie typed it into her laptop. It went like this:

When an important new
invention comes into being,
whether it is the telegraph,
the telephone, or the
television, the only thing
that can be said for sure is
that it will bring change.
Which brings us to the subject
of this report: Computers—
good news or bad news?

"Well, it's a start," said Bonnie.

"I guess so," said Brother. He sat back in his chair and looked around the squire's study. It was very special—like the rest of the rooms in the mansion. It had polished wood paneling and tall shelves of leather-bound books. There was even a little ladder on wheels so you could reach the books on the top shelves.

"Bonnie," said Brother, "what is it like having the richest bear in Bear Country for your uncle?" There was a knock at the door.

"Come in," said Bonnie. It was Greeves, the butler.

"The squire directed me to bring you a bit of supper," he said. "It's cheeseburgers, Miss."

"Thank you, Greeves," said Bonnie. "I'll tell you what it's like," she said to Brother. "It's like having the richest bear in Bear Country for your uncle."

Chapter 8
Babs Is a Hit!

After much thought and some nervousness, Babs chose "Fog" to be her first poem in cyberspace. It was a chat room hit. There was always a critique after the first poem by a new member. Babs glowed with pride as the compliments came in thick and fast:

Terrific! Let's have more!

You are a great addition to the Young Poets chat room.

Way to go, Goldiebear!

But Babs decided to stop while she was ahead. She typed a thank-you into cyberspace.

```
Thank you! Thank you! That's
enough from me for now. I want
to see some of your poems.
                Goldiebear
```

The Young Poets chat room warmed up quickly and poems came on screen in a steady stream. All kinds of poems! One young poet, nicknamed Rhymester, specialized in limericks.

```
There once was a teacher named Mamie
who taught every subject the samie.
Her style was a bore.
Her students did snore.
For inducing sleep, she won acclaimie.
```

Wow! thought Babs. I'd like to see Rhymester publish that in his school paper! That was another thing about cyberspace. Nobody knew who you were. Nobody even knew whether you were a boy or a girl. Babs decided right then and there to print out every poem that came on-line. She would make them into a book called *Poems from Cyberspace* and maybe hand it in for extra credit. Then there was "Spooky," who specialized in scary poems.

> In the dark in the park
> there are hideous moans.
> In the dark in the park
> there are skeleton bones
> slithering out from under
> the stones.

While Babs was trying to figure out whether Spooky was a boy or girl, another

poem came on screen. It was signed "Puff."
It was the young poet who had already
taken that name!

> Our plans are humming.
> The time is coming.
> He's had time enough.
> The time has come to
>   Huff and Puff.
>   —Puff

It wasn't much of a poem. It was more
like a message. And sure enough, an
answering poem followed, and it was signed
"Huff."

```
Message received
and understood.
We're going to get SG
and get him good!
              —Huff
```

Babs wondered about Huff and Puff. She started to wonder who SG was, but then her mom called her to come down and set the table and get ready for dinner. Later that evening, she would go back to her room and rejoin the Young Poets chat room.

After printing out more poems, she washed up, put on her pajamas, and climbed into bed—and watched the Young Poets chat room. It was sort of like reading in bed after lights out. Only instead of a book and a flashlight, she had a laptop with a glowing screen. After a while, she drifted off to sleep with the laptop and the printer still on.

Chapter 9
A Stud in His Nose

"He said he was very tall and he'd be wearing a really sharp suit, a wide-brimmed hat, and a stud in his nose," said Bermuda as she scanned the busy Pizza Shack scene. "Do you see anybody that looks like that?"

"Nope," said Queenie. "Let's go home."

"Wait. I see somebody coming out of the shadows that might fit that description," said Bermuda. "Yep. I think it's your computer date. Tall, sharp suit, wide-brimmed hat, nose stud. The whole gorgeous package. Here he comes. Well, don't just stand there! Go meet and greet the guy."

But Queenie just froze. And when the computer date came close, he froze, too—and stared. After a long silence he spoke. His voice was familiar.

"Queenie?" he said. "Is that you behind that weird makeup, those crazy clothes, and that purple nail polish?"

It took Queenie a long second to find her voice. "Too-Tall?" she said. "Is that you in that weird hat, that crazy suit, and that nose stud?"

"It's just a pastie," said Too-Tall, flicking it off.

"What is this?" said Bermuda angrily. "Have you two been putting me on?"

"No way!" protested Queenie. "You talked me into the idea of computer-dating an older guy. And now I'm talking myself out of it."

"That's what happened to me," said Too-Tall. "The gang dared me to computer-date an older girl. Naturally, I had to take the dare. So I borrowed these clothes from Vinnie's older brother. The nose stud came in a

box of cereal. Okay, gang, you can come out now!"

Skuzz, Smirk, and Vinnie stepped out of the shadows. The three of them were doubled over with laughter. Soon Queenie and Too-Tall were too. Even Bermuda realized it was funny. Though, in a way, the joke was on her.

"Hey, guys," said Queenie. "Let's go over to the Burger Bear for burgers and fries."

And that's what happened. Queenie and the guys headed for the Burger Bear, and Bermuda blended into the Pizza Shack crowd.

Chapter 10
Cyberspace Emergency

As it turned out, Babs fell asleep with her laptop on. It ran all night, and a thick pile of printouts ended up in the holder. She started going through them at breakfast. It was just Babs and her mom at breakfast. Her dad had been called away early.

She continued to look through them on her way to school. There was the usual run of poems, and some of them were pretty good. The idea of collecting them in a book called *Poems from Cyberspace* was looking better and better. But then she came to another exchange between Puff and Huff. And then *another* exchange between Puff and Huff. She stopped dead in her tracks. Her eyes opened wide as she read. She broke into a run.

She was completely out of breath when she reached the schoolyard, where Queenie was telling the rest of the gang about her big computer date. "Oh, come on," said Bonnie.

"No, it really happened," said Queenie. "And I've got the purple fingernails to prove it." She held out her nails.

"Good grief," said Bonnie.

"Hey, here comes Babs, puffing like a steam engine," said Brother. "Something must be wrong."

At first all Babs could manage to do was gasp for breath and wave the stack of print-outs. But finally she caught her breath enough to squeeze out, "Emergency! Some kind of big crime is coming down on the Internet!"

Brother took a quick look at the Huff and Puff printouts. "I don't know what this is about. But it looks serious. Come on! We've got to show this to Teacher Bob."

But the bell hadn't rung yet and the door safety wouldn't let them in. "But it's an emergency!" cried Babs.

"What sort of emergency?" said the door safety.

"It's going to be an emergency for your nose if you don't let us in," said Too-Tall. The door safety let them in.

"What's going on?" demanded Teacher Bob as the gang stormed into the room.

"Babs picked this up off the Internet last night," said Brother, thrusting the printouts at Teacher Bob. "There's some sort of crime coming down on the Young Poets chat room."

Teacher Bob smiled. "C'mon," he said. "Don't you think the idea of a crime coming down on the Young Poets chat room is a little…"

"Read it, please!" Brother laid all six poems out on Teacher Bob's desk.

"Oh, my," said Teacher Bob. He read the poems aloud:

Our plans are humming.
The time is coming.
He's had time enough.
The time has come to
Huff and Puff.
                    —Puff

Message received
and understood.
We're going to get SG
and get him good!
                    —Huff

The letters SG jumped out at Teacher Bob and the class. "SG! That's got to be Squire Grizzly," said Brother. "It looks like it's about Bonnie's uncle, Squire Grizzly, and Grizzly Mansion."

"Oh, my poor uncle!" cried Bonnie.

Teacher Bob read on:

The time has come
to deliver the note.
Look out for the guards.
Look out for the moat.
—Puff

We are ready,
ready to go,
ready and willing
to strike our blow.
—Huff

"That's *got* to be about Grizzly Mansion!" cried Brother. "It's the only place in Bear Country with a moat."

"And just listen to this!" said Teacher Bob.

So leave your package
at the midnight hour!
Hail, all hail
computer power!
        —Puff

We will huff and puff
and blow his house down.
We will blow his house
all over town!
        —Huff

"We've got to do something!" cried Bonnie.

"I'm already doing it," said Babs. "I'm putting in a call to my dad." Teacher Bob and the class gathered around.

"But it's an emergency, Officer Marguerite! I've got to talk to him!" Babs looked up from the phone. "She says he can't come to the phone. He's got an emergency, too."

Teacher Bob grabbed the phone. "This is Teacher Bob, Officer Marguerite! We've got

information about a crime—a threat to Grizzly Mansion! It was picked up on the Internet, and we've got the printouts to prove it!" He paused to listen. "Okay! Okay! Will do!" He crashed the phone down and said, "They're dealing with the same emergency! They want us at the police station right away with these printouts."

The cubs all poured into Teacher Bob's minivan, and off they roared crosstown to the police station.

Chapter 11
Demand for Money by Threat

What impressed the cubs about the police station was that even though there was a big crime in progress, everything was calm—tense and businesslike, but calm. Officer Marguerite took them into a room that had a projector and a screen. The chief came in. Teacher Bob handed Chief Bruno the printouts. The chief looked through them quickly. "And you printed these off the Internet, Babs?" he said.

"That's right, Dad," said Babs.

"Wow," said the chief. "This looks like the real thing. It might even help break the case. All we've got so far is the note. Put it up on the screen, Marguerite."

This is what it said:

```
Dear Squire Grizzly,
Please leave one million
dollars in unmarked bills in
the old hollow stump by the
auto graveyard. If you do as
we say, you and yours will
be safe. If you do not, you
and yours will be sorry.
```

"What do you make of it, Chief?" asked Teacher Bob.

"Well, we didn't know what to make of it until you brought these in. But it's clear from these printouts that we're dealing with extortion: a demand for money by threat. We're not getting much out of the note, but these will give us something to work with."

"But what about my aunt and uncle?" asked Bonnie.

"They're perfectly safe," said the chief. "They've moved into one of the squire's hotels. They and their entire staff have taken over the top two floors. Security at the hotel is one hundred percent. That's where you'll be living until we deal with this threat.

"Also, I've called a SWAT team in from Big Bear City. They know their business. But it's our case. Come on into the computer room and I'll show you how the police use computers."

Chapter 12
Perps in Cyberspace

The chief sat down in front of the police computer setup. It was a lot bigger than a laptop. It had three screens and two printers, and it was tied into a fax machine. "Now, these perps are lost somewhere out there in cyberspace," said the chief.

"Perps. That's police talk for 'perpetrators,'" explained Babs.

"Thank you, Babs," said Chief Bruno. "And it's our job to find them. Now, we're pretty sure from Babs's printouts that we're dealing with a couple of extortionists who are communicating over the Internet. One of them calls himself Puff and one calls himself Huff. Or maybe it's a whole gang of extortionists."

"Why do you suppose they're using the Internet to communicate?" asked Teacher Bob.

"It's hard to say," said the chief. "Maybe one of them is the mastermind and stays far from the action. Or, maybe, they're afraid of phone taps. You can't tap the Internet. Actually, the Internet is a pretty safe place for criminals. It was a zillion-to-one chance that Babs picked up their traffic on the Young Poets chat room. But I've got to get to work. We've got to start somewhere."

He typed the word E-X-T-O-R-T-I-O-N-I-S-T. In a flash, a list of names popped onto the screen.

```
Buzz Grizwire
Sam Smith
Moose Brack
Frank Murdock
Butch Bearstow
Ugly Bear Johnson
Fingers Finagle
Bill (the Thug) Barr
J. Arthur Bruin
Stickpin McGuffin
```

"Those are the top ten extortionists. There's no telling if our subjects are among them. So let's check into their modus operandi. That's Latin for 'mode of operation,' which should tell the method each of them uses to extort money."

The chief typed in M-O-D-U-S O-P-E-R-A-N-D-I. Immediately words appeared beside each of the names.

Buzz Grizwire	blackmailer
Sam Smith	blackmailer
Moose Brack	direct assault
Frank Murdock	direct assault
Butch Bearstow	cubnapper
Ugly Bear Johnson	bomber
Fingers Finagle	cubnapper
Bill (the Thug) Barr	bomber
J. Arthur Bruin	bomber
Stickpin McGuffin	bomber

"Wow!" whispered Barry. "It's a regular jungle out there."

"Shh," said Teacher Bob. "I want to hear the chief."

"It's clear from Babs's printouts that we're probably looking at a bomb plot here," said the chief. "So let's knock out everybody but the bombers." A few keystrokes, and all that was left on the screen were the bombers.

```
Ugly Bear Johnson
Bill (the Thug) Barr
J. Arthur Bruin
Stickpin McGuffin
```

WOW! IT'S A REGULAR JUNGLE OUT THERE.

"Now, there's no way to be sure," said the chief, "but our perps could be there. Hmm, let's have a look at any aliases they might have. Those are other names they go by to avoid getting caught. I'm going to type in a.k.a., which stands for 'also known as.'"

And this is what came up on the screen!

Ugly Bear Johnson
   Flat Face, Double Nose
Bill (the Thug) Barr
   No known aliases
J. Arthur Bruin
   Lord Huff 'n Puff
Stickpin McGuffin
   Slick, the Guff

"Look! Look!" shouted the cubs. "You've got 'im! That J. Arthur Bruin guy!"

The chief stared at the screen. "How about that! It sure ties in with all that Huff

and Puff stuff in the printouts. I don't know if we're there yet. But we sure are on our way. Let's see if we can find out more about this J. Arthur Bruin, a.k.a. Lord Huff 'n Puff."

The chief typed in the phrase K-N-O-W-N W-H-E-R-E-A-B-O-U-T-S. What came up on the screen was a shock.

```
Known whereabouts of subject,
J. Arthur Bruin, a.k.a. Lord
Huff 'n Puff: presently
serving eight-year sentence
at Bear Country State Prison
for extortion. Convicted in
remote-control bombing of Bear
Country First National Bank.
Head of Huff 'n Puff gang.
Highly intelligent. Has expert
knowledge of computers.
Further information on wanted
members of Huff 'n Puff gang
available upon request.
```

"Wow!" said Brother.

"You can say that again!" said the chief.

This time all the cubs joined in. "WOW!"

Chapter 13
Bonnie Breaks Down

After that, it was mostly a matter of careful police work. But without Babs's printouts, the police might never have solved the case. Chief Bruno admitted as much. He admitted it right there on the television news.

"Shh, cubs, I want to hear the chief," said Teacher Bob. It was the next day, and he had brought a television into the classroom.

"Chief," said the anchorbear, "are we to understand that it was some computer printouts that broke the case?"

"That's correct," said the chief. "All we had was the extortion note. And while we might have been able to trace the note, it would have been a very tough job and it might have been too late to prevent a terrible crime."

"And is it true that it was Teacher Bob's class at Bear Country School that picked up on the computer traffic that solved the case?"

"That's correct," said the chief.

A cheer went up from the class. "Shh," said Teacher Bob.

"And," continued the anchor, "that it was your very own daughter, Babs Bruno, who found that traffic on the Young Poets chat room? Have I got that right—the Young Poets chat room?"

"You've got it right," said the chief with a glow of pride. "It was quite a scheme, really. It turns out this Bruin fellow is a real computer expert. So much so that he was put in charge of the whole prison computer system."

"But wasn't he supervised?" asked the anchor.

"Well," said the chief, "the prison listens in on all phone calls and all talks between prisoners and visitors, but it's pretty hard to supervise a computer. It takes just seconds to get messages out over the Internet. And the Young Poets chat room was a perfect cover."

"What's going to happen to this criminal computer genius?" asked the anchor.

"I think it's fair to say that his sentence will be extended and his computer privileges will be taken away."

"I also understand, Chief, that you've caught the entire gang. Can you tell us about that?"

"I'm afraid that's classified," said the chief.

"Thank you very much, Chief Bruno," said the anchor, turning to the camera. "You have been listening to…"

Teacher Bob switched off the television. "Did your dad tell you what happened, Babs?"

"Yeah! Yeah! Tell us! Tell us!" clamored the class.

YEAH! YEAH! TELL US! TELL US!

"Here's what I know," said Babs. "His SWAT team caught Huff—he was the outside guy, Puff was the inside guy—in the moat with a remote-control bomb in his backpack. Then they caught the rest of the gang waiting in a getaway car up the road."

As you might expect, the members of Teacher Bob's class felt very good about themselves that day—and very close. They were congratulating each other all over the place. Even Too-Tall and Ferdy Factual were exchanging bear hugs. Brother turned to congratulate Bonnie, but she had separated herself from the class. She was sitting in a corner of the room—crying.

"What is it, Bonnie?" asked Brother.

"What's the matter?"

"Oh, I don't know," said Bonnie. Queenie gave her a hanky for her tears. "When I think of what might have happened if Babs hadn't visited the Young Poets chat room and if she didn't just *happen* to fall asleep with the printer on and if Babs's dad didn't just *happen* to be chief of police…" Bonnie put her face in her hands and was crying hard. Brother felt awful. He didn't know what to do. Queenie and Babs did their best to comfort her. But it was Too-Tall who broke the crying cycle.

"You know what I say about this whole crazy business?" said Too-Tall. "I say thank goodness for co-inky-dinks!" That brought Bonnie's smile back.

Then the class tried to get back to regular schoolwork. They didn't succeed very well. But they tried.

REPORT CARD
TOO-TALL GRIZZLY

ENGLISH............ D
MATH............... E
HISTORY............ D-
ART................ D+
SHOP............... C-
PHYS. ED........... C+

Chapter 14
The End of an Experiment

As for Squire Grizzly's big laptop experiment, it was canceled after less than two weeks. The whole idea of the experiment was to find out if computers would help the cubs with their education, to find out if computers would help the test class improve their grades. But the opposite happened. Instead of their grades getting better, they got worse. Of course, certain students—Ferdy, Trudy, and Bonnie, for example—continued to get straight A's. But the rest of the class went down. Even Brother, who had always been at least a B student, went down to C. As for Too-Tall and the gang, their marks were *underwater*.

The reason was obvious. It was clear to Teacher Bob that most of the class spent so much time on their laptops with chat rooms, computer games, web sites, and goodness knows what else, they didn't have any time left over for schoolwork. Teacher Bob didn't want to be a pill about it. He wasn't against fun. And he certainly wasn't against computers. He thought computers were marvelous—for certain things: number crunching, research, organizing information—and fun, too. But education was the purpose of the experiment, not fun. So Teacher Bob had a meeting with Squire Grizzly and Mr. Honeycomb. "It's not that I'm against computers," he told them. "Quite the contrary. I'm convinced they can be very important in educating cubs. But I don't think handing them out willy-nilly is the answer."

"But what about the expense I've gone to?" asked Squire Grizzly. "What about all those laptops I've purchased?"

"The squire has a point," said the principal. "And he's been very generous."

"He has indeed," said Teacher Bob. "And I'm going to ask him to be even more generous. Here's my suggestion. Squire, why don't you trade those laptops in and purchase an even bigger number of regular PC's? Then we can set up a really super computer lab, with enough computers so that each cub can use one for an hour a day."

"That sounds like a pretty good plan," said the squire. "But how about your students? Won't they be disappointed?"

"Sure," said Teacher Bob. "But disappointment is a part of life. And besides, I think they'll make the best of it."

And they did. One morning, a couple of weeks after the laptops were taken back, Teacher Bob was looking out his classroom window. It was almost time for the bell to ring and the school day to start. And while all wasn't necessarily right with the world, things had gotten back to normal after the excitement and tension of the laptop experiment. Brother was playing ball with Cousin Fred, Queenie was telling Babs and Bonnie the latest bit of gossip, Barry was trying out his latest bad joke on some poor unfortunate, and Too-Tall and his gang were swaggering through the schoolyard frightening kindergartners.

And that weekend, the whole gang went to the movies together. Brother and Bonnie sat away from the others and held hands.

Stan and Jan Berenstain began writing and illustrating books for children in the early 1960s, when their two young sons were beginning to read. That marked the start of the best-selling Berenstain Bears series. Now, with more than one hundred books in print, videos, television shows, and even Berenstain Bears attractions at major amusement parks, it's hard to tell where the Bears end and the Berenstains begin!

Stan and Jan make their home in Bucks County, Pennsylvania, near their sons—Leo, a writer, and Michael, an illustrator—who are helping them with Big Chapter Books stories and pictures. They plan on writing and illustrating many more books for children, especially for their four grandchildren, who keep them well in touch with the kids of today.